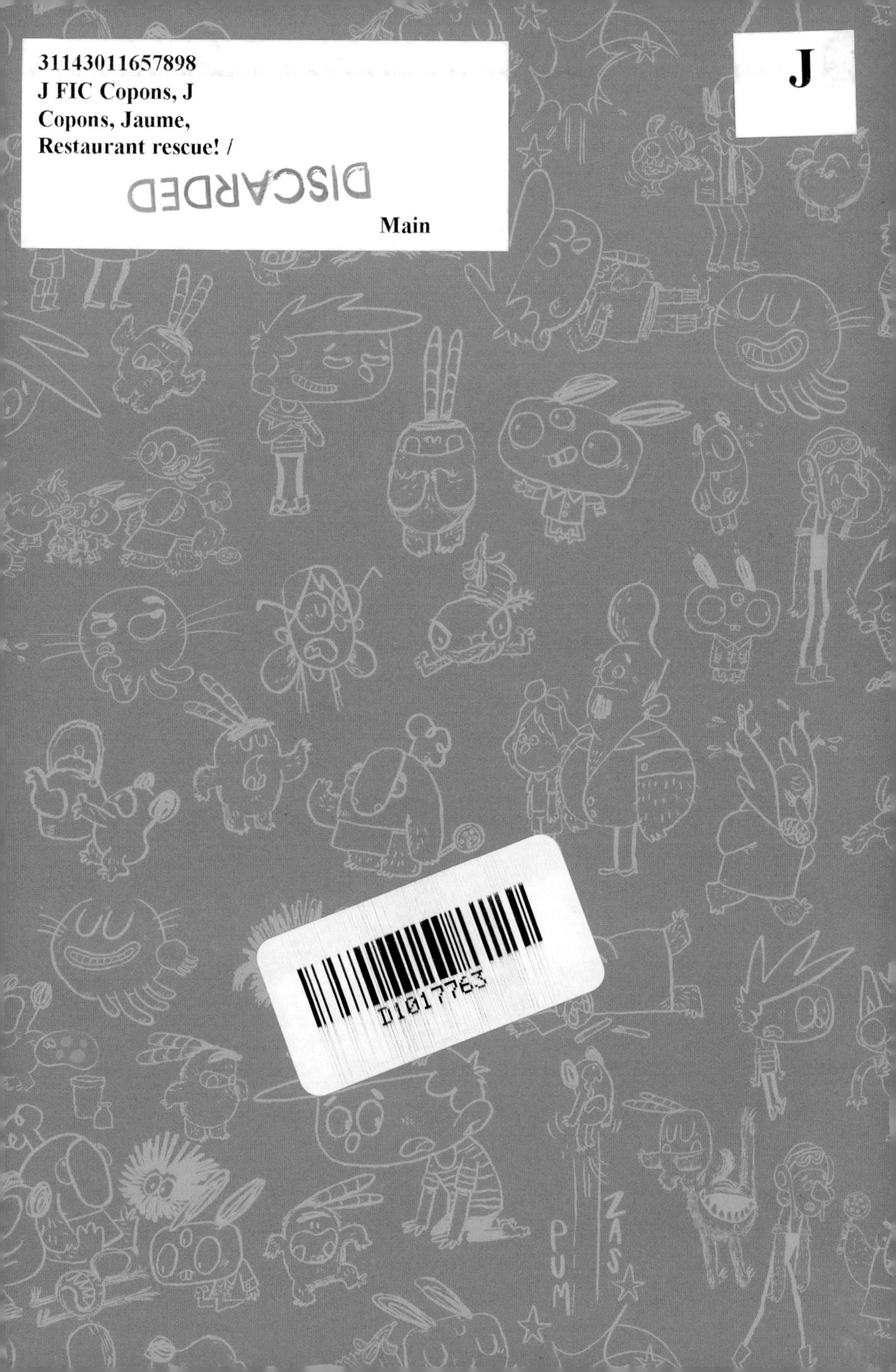
PUM
ZAS

RESTAURANT RESCUE!

JAUME COPONS AND
LILIANA FORTUNY

Translated from the French by David Warriner

CRACKBOOM!

1

A bedroom full of monsters

I don't really care that the teacher has given us such a weird assignment. I have a week of vacation ahead of me and I'm going to spend it all with my friends anyway. Homework doesn't bother me much.

After school, I walk home with Lidia. I don't really have any choice because we're neighbors. We're such close neighbors we even live on the same floor of the building. It really is too bad, because Lidia's the worst gossip in the whole school. And don't even get me started about her dad.

Once I've got away from Lidia and her dad, I can finally go back into my place, say hi to my parents and go straight to my room, because that's where my friends are waiting. They're a little strange, but I wouldn't trade them for anything in the world. Sometimes they go a little over the top, for sure, but they just can't help themselves!

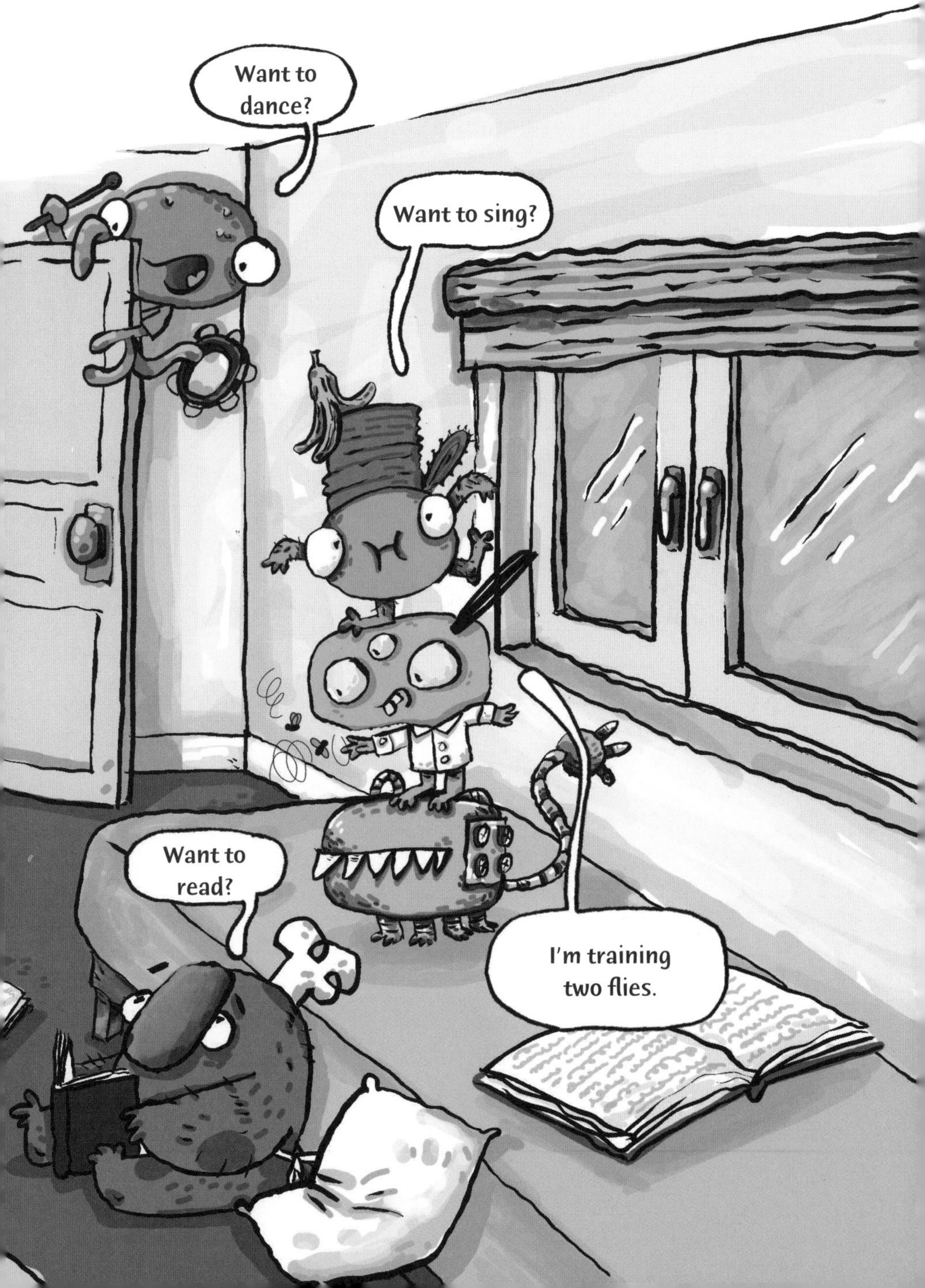
Want to dance?
Want to sing?
Want to read?
I'm training two flies.

Before we can play and read, though, we have some work to do! I have to tidy my room. It isn't easy living with ten monsters! It takes a lot of discipline. And above all, it's important to keep the place tidy to avoid arousing suspicion. Fortunately, Mr. Flat helps out a little with his organizational skills.

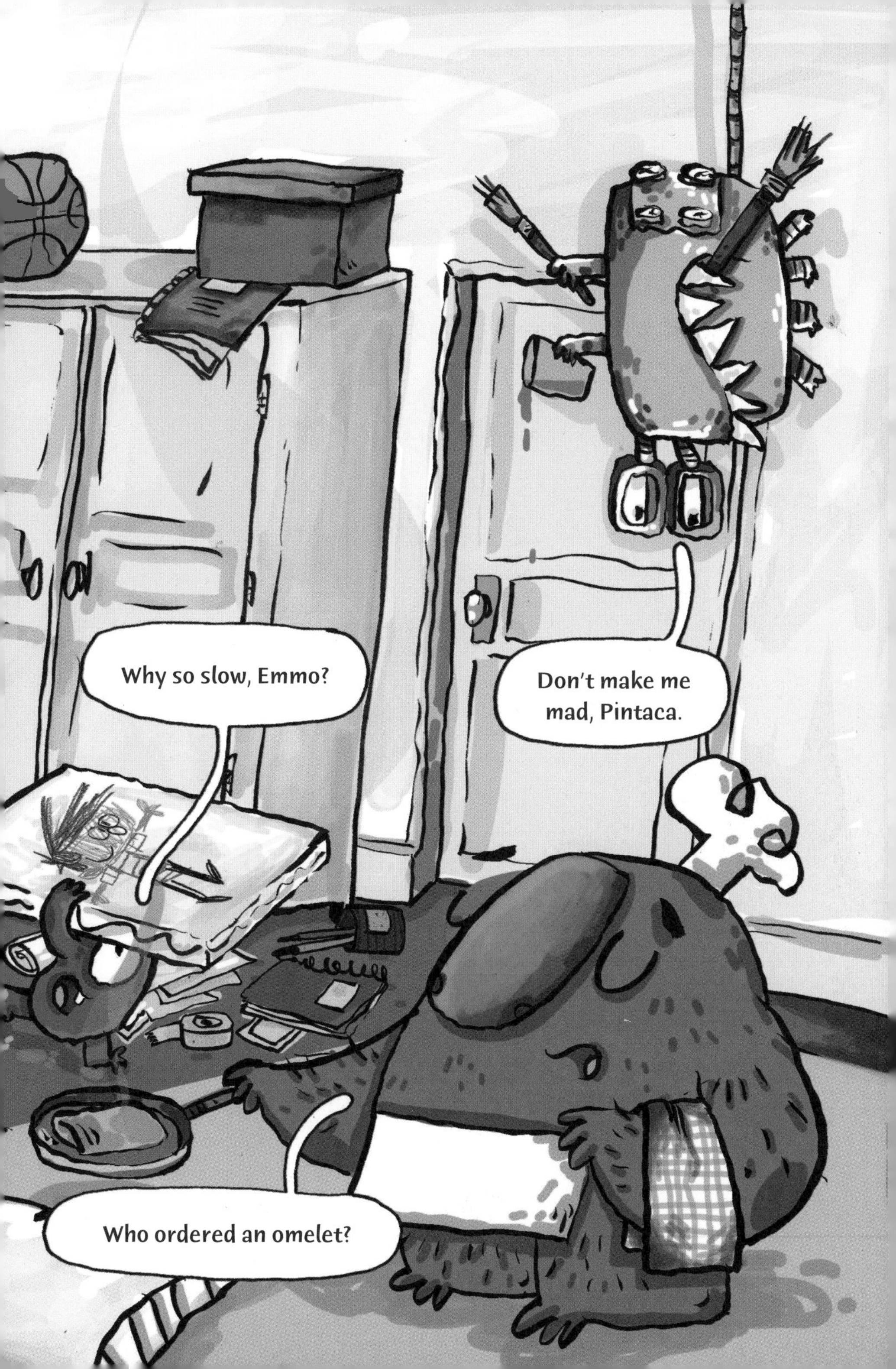
Why so slow, Emmo?
Don't make me mad, Pintaca.
Who ordered an omelet?

Keeping your room tidy avoids a whole bunch of problems. If your parents come into your room and see everything's tidy, usually they won't suspect a thing. But I suppose there are some parents, like mine, who always find something to complain about.

These ten monsters and I have been sharing my bedroom for the last three weeks. I think I should explain how I ended up getting to know them. That way, you'll see why I have every interest in keeping my room tidy.

HOW MR. FLAT AND THE MONSTERS CAME TO LIVE IN MY ROOM

I used to be just a regular kid, with the regular kind of problems a regular kid has. The usual stuff, like my mom threatening to throw away my toys if I didn't tidy my room. I had a problem at school too. I needed to hand in my written assignments to the teacher, but I had lost them.

One day, I found Mr. Flat at the library and I thought he was a stuffed toy. Emma, the librarian, gave him to me.

Later that day, I started reading a story and Mr. Flat woke up. He wasn't a stuffed toy after all, he was the book monster! We instantly became friends and read loads of books together. But …

… Mr. Flat told me how he and his friends had been chased out of the book they were living in, *The Book of Monsters*, by a very mean man called Dr. Brut. I decided to help Mr. Flat.

The next day, things grew more complicated. My mom, who was tired of nagging me about the mess in my room, got rid of a lot of my toys, and Mr. Flat was one of them.

After a few twists and turns and plenty of discussion with Lidia, who had bought Mr. Flat from the toy stall at school where my mom had taken him, I was finally reunited with my new friend.

Back at home, Mr. Flat miraculously found all my written work that I had to hand in to my class teacher. And he made a proposal …

He suggested his friends should come live with us. Needless to say, I was happy to accept!

Since the monsters moved into my bedroom, we haven't been bored for a single second. At night, Mr. Flat and I read out loud together while all the others listen to us in awe. We lead a pretty fun and quiet life, but ...

As we're tidying up my room, I realize Drilox and Krater are nowhere to be found. And when I ask where they are, the others pretend they don't know a thing.

2

Trouble with the neighbors

Even though my attempts to find Drilox and Krater fall on deaf ears with the other monsters, I'm not in the dark for long. A hole suddenly opens up in the wall and the two missing monsters emerge into my room. I can't believe what I'm seeing. Fortunately, Krater, the hole monster, doesn't just know how to make a hole, he also knows how to put things back the way they were.

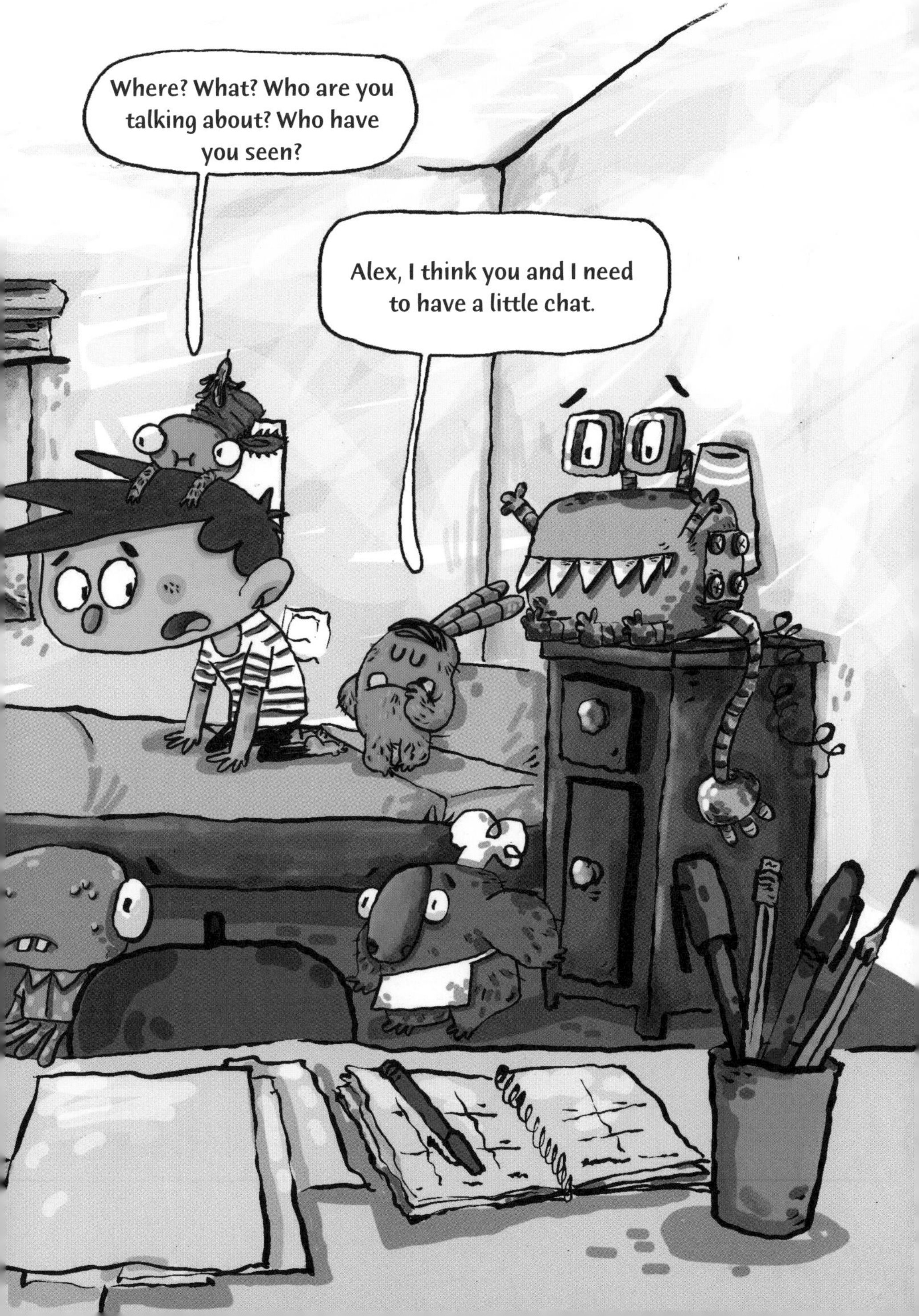
Where? What? Who are you talking about? Who have you seen?
Alex, I think you and I need to have a little chat.

And so, Mr. Flat and I talk for a moment. He explains it's no coincidence he and the other monsters have ended up in my room. Since they were banished from *The Book of Monsters*, they've been searching everywhere for Dr. Brut.

My very first thought is that we have to get *The Book of Monsters* back, by hook or by crook, so my friends can live there again.

I know we have to get *The Book of Monsters* back, but I soon realize it's not going to be as easy as I thought.

The monsters explain that they all want to stop Dr. Brut from going through with his evil plans. They say we'll have to be patient, though, and wait for him to mess up. Personally, it seems clear to me that we need to stay on our guard, especially given the way they've been talking about Dr. Brut!

Okay, so Dr. Brut is a dangerous man. But what about Nabo, Dr. Brut's sidekick? The monsters are a little more vague about him. What little they do say isn't much help.

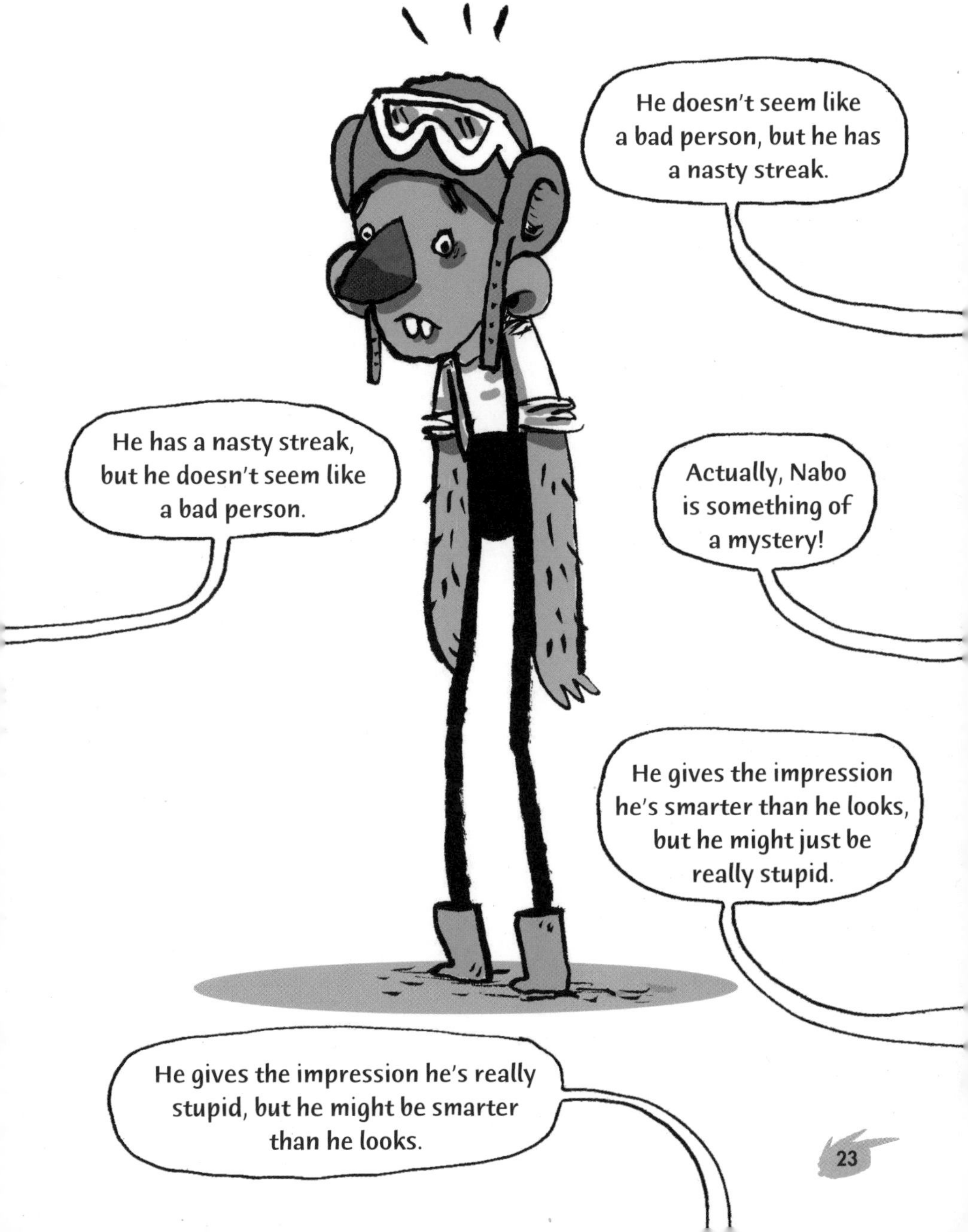

He doesn't seem like a bad person, but he has a nasty streak.
He has a nasty streak, but he doesn't seem like a bad person.
Actually, Nabo is something of a mystery!
He gives the impression he's smarter than he looks, but he might just be really stupid.
He gives the impression he's really stupid, but he might be smarter than he looks.

Ziro starts calculating what Dr. Brut is likely to do next, but I don't think he really knows what he's doing. Honestly, I find Ziro's calculations totally incomprehensible. Anyhow, I'm starting to realize, after three weeks with these monsters, that sometimes they act in the most bizarre and strangest possible ways. But they always end up figuring things out!

That night, Mr. Flat and I read *Alice in Wonderland*, by Lewis Carroll. In complete and utter silence, all the other monsters listen to us recount Alice's adventures in Wonderland. Well, silence is a bit of an exaggeration, actually.

We read for a good while before my dad comes in and interrupts. It's late and we have to turn out the light. While he's in my room, the monsters freeze and don't move a muscle, as if they were stuffies. They're used to doing that. When my dad leaves the room, we're able to keep reading pretty easily thanks to Emmo and his bright ideas.

We read until it's super late because we're all enthralled by Alice. And because we want to know how the trial ends!

As we're reading, Octosol has a little accident. He wants to pretend he's Alice falling down the rabbit hole, so he jumps off the top of the wardrobe. But the poor little monster hurts himself when he hits the floor.

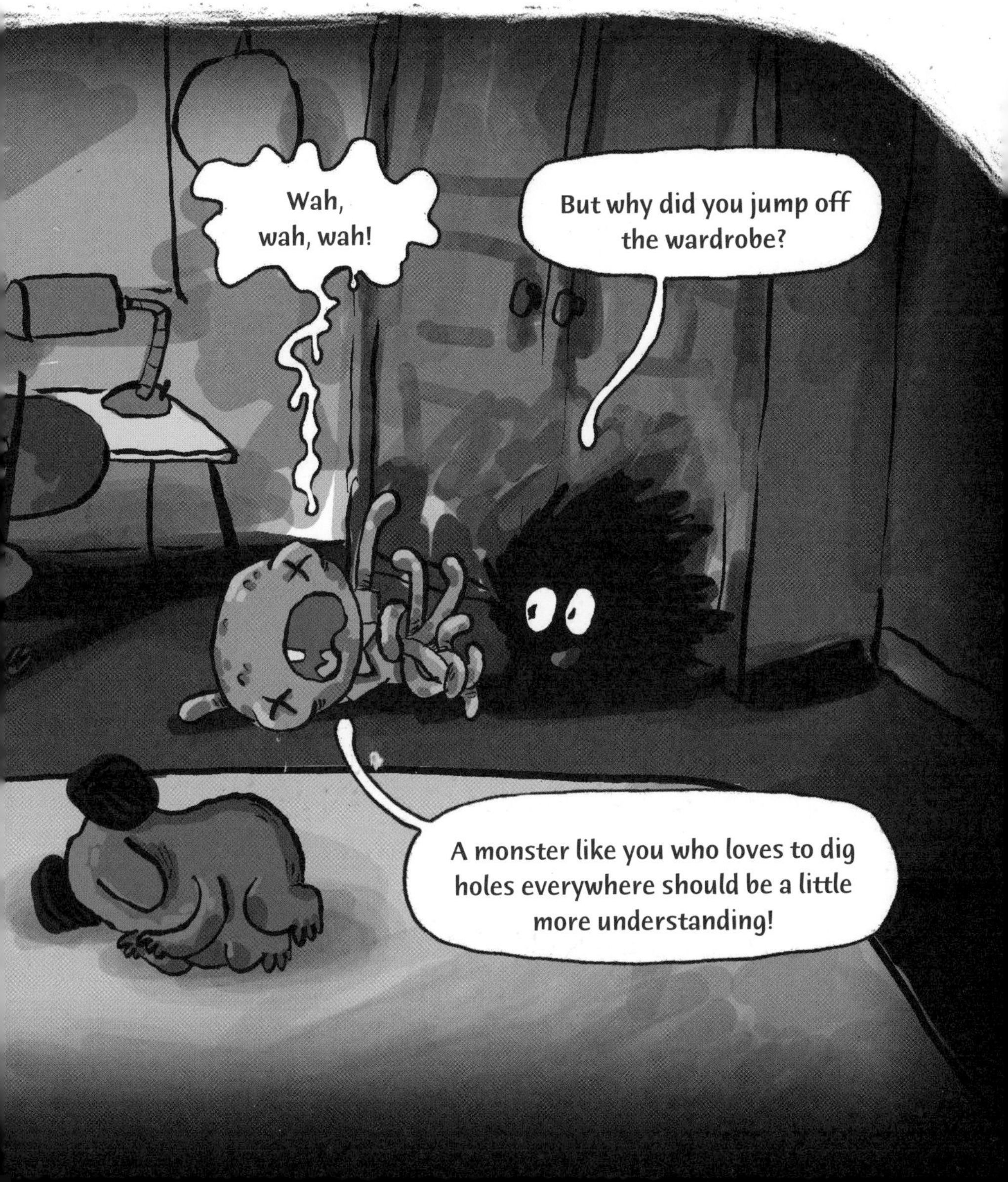
Wah, wah, wah!
But why did you jump off the wardrobe?
A monster like you who loves to dig holes everywhere should be a little more understanding!

3

Playing detective

As soon as we wake up, we get down to work. We decide to do a little investigating in the park. How can we make sure nobody out there sees the monsters, though? I suggest I carry them in a big backpack. Krater tells me there's no need.

Krater's really hard to follow! Even if we make a hole in the bag, there's not enough room for all the monsters. Still, as strange as it might seem, they all manage to fit.

My parents are over the moon to hear I'm going to the park. They find I've been spending too much time in my room lately. I think my dad's even quite proud to see his son becoming more responsible, like a true Pianola.

Five minutes later, I'm sitting on a park bench with my friends. Or rather, I'm sitting on a park bench, and the monsters are safe and sound at the very bottom of the hole in my bag Krater made. And guess who I run into at the park?

Thanks to my thrilling conversation skills, Lidia gets bored after less than a minute and goes away. We decide to get up and move over to another bench right in front of the house in the park.

Suddenly, we see them! Dr. Brut is coming out of the treehouse, and Nabo is there too. I freeze on the bench as they walk right past us.

Mr. Flat asks me to follow Dr. Brut, so I get up right away.

I follow Dr. Brut's every footstep. He doesn't even realize I'm there. When he stops, I stop. When he walks, I walk.

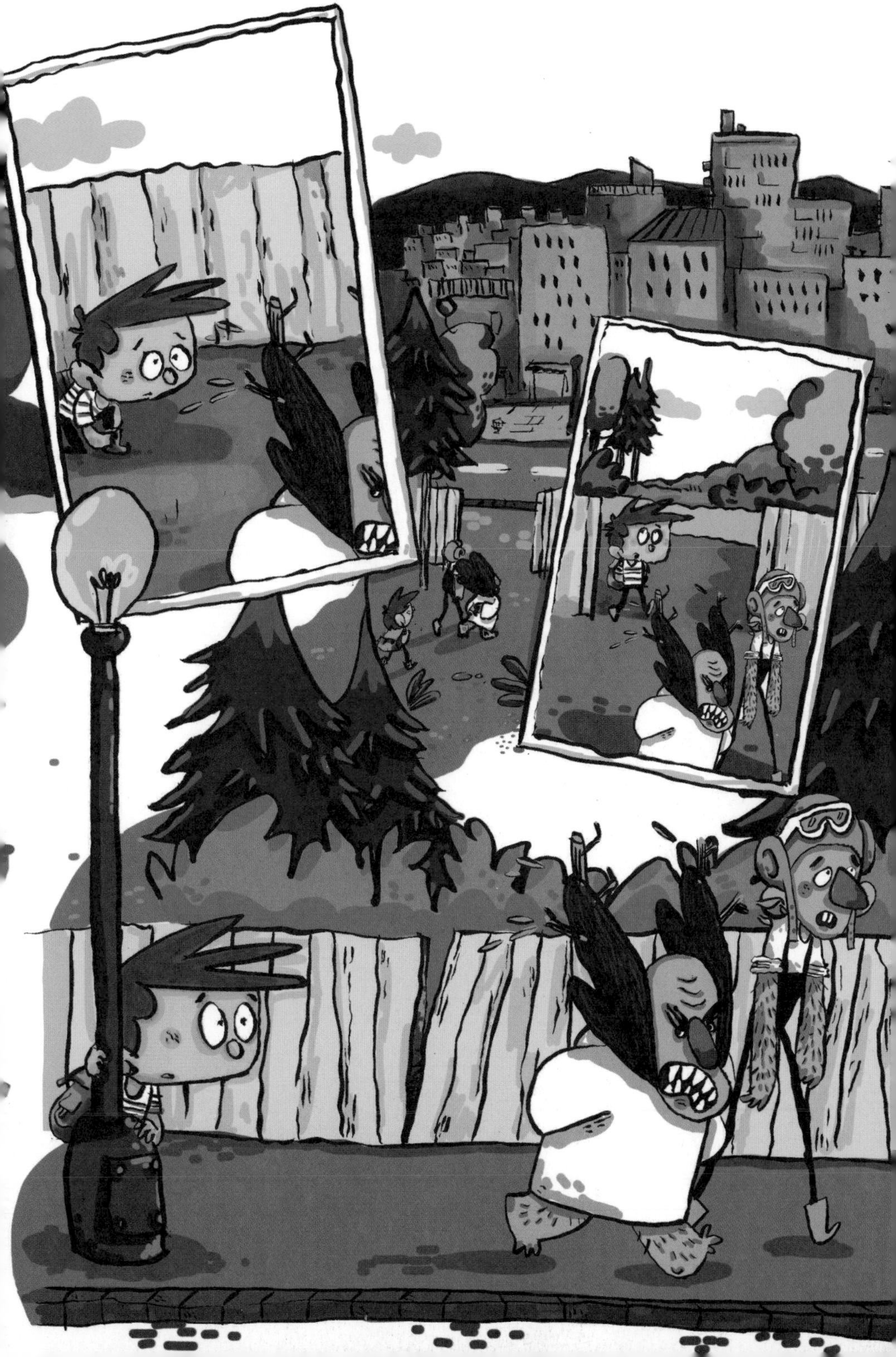

Dr. Brut and Nabo walk out of the park, and suddenly they stop in front of a restaurant very close to where I live. I stop too. In spite of the monsters complaining in my bag, I inch my way a little closer to the dastardly duo so I can hear what they're saying.

I put my bag down for a moment. Even though the monsters are in a hole, they're still very heavy! We wait around on the street while Dr. Brut and Nabo are eating inside the restaurant.

Nabo lazily throws the newspaper on the sidewalk. We pick it up, of course. Surely it must hold some clues about what's cooking.

And there, standing in the street, we understand what's happening when we open the newspaper.

CULTURE

JEAN-PAUL SORBET TO VISIT THE NAUTILUS

A dreaded review from the most discerning of gastronomes

Jean-Paul Sorbet in a recent photograph.

This November 22, the renowned gourmet restaurant critic Jean-Paul Sorbet will be paying a visit to the Nautilus restaurant here in our city. His visits are renowned for propelling restaurants to great success or ruining them completely. The famous gastronome's reviews are published in the world's most prestigious newspapers, gourmet food guides and foodie blogs. Restaurant owner Ody Jules said, "We know our reputation is on the line here." His wife Penelope Verne added, "We're going to do our best to show what a grand restaurant the Nautilus is." That said, nothing is a foregone conclusion. In recent months, the Nautilus has lost its shine and plenty of customers too. This November 22, the future of the Nautilus restaurant could be decided by the toss of a coin.

4

A plan for
the Nautilus

It's obvious what Dr. Brut is planning to do. He wants to go to the restaurant on the same day as Jean-Paul Sorbet to make sure things go badly. When we're safely back home, in spite of the excitement of seeing Dr. Brut with our own eyes, we start to draw up our plan.

It's simple. Dr. Brut is going to try to make the owners of the Nautilus look bad.

We have to act fast! And we have to use this opportunity to find out where our book is!.

Alex could go to the restaurant and bring a few of us along, so we know exactly what's going on.

We all agree on one thing very quickly. Since the Nautilus is a restaurant, the most logical choice would be to send Chef Roll to the rescue. But he doesn't see it that way.

It's decided. Chef Roll will be going to the restaurant. And all the other monsters agree I should be the one to take him there. Mr. Flat irons out the details. He suggests I go in disguise, so nobody will recognize me and I can go back another time without a problem.

Alex, you can just leave Chef Roll at the restaurant and then turn around and walk out of there, no problem. Go on, look for a costume in your dress-up chest!

I have no idea what I can dress up as!

We dig around in my costume chest for a long time before we find something suitable.

Eventually, we decide the best disguise is for me to dress up as an old granny. Who would bat an eye at a little old lady?

Because Krater is so good at making holes, he's going to come along with Chef Roll. That way, they can get out of the restaurant easily and make their way home.

Once I'm in my disguise, I carry Chef Roll and Krater over to the restaurant, but I stumble across an obstacle I should have seen coming. As soon as I set foot outside, I run into the last people I want to see. Argh!

Fortunately, Lidia and her dad are in a hurry. They don't hold me up for long.

Once I arrive at the Nautilus, I go inside and put Chef Roll on a stool. I ask for a glass of water and, while it's being poured, I make a run for it.

While we're waiting for Chef Roll and Krater to get back from the Nautilus, the monsters and I form two teams for a quick game of Brexfest. Brexfest is a super fun sport that Brex invented.

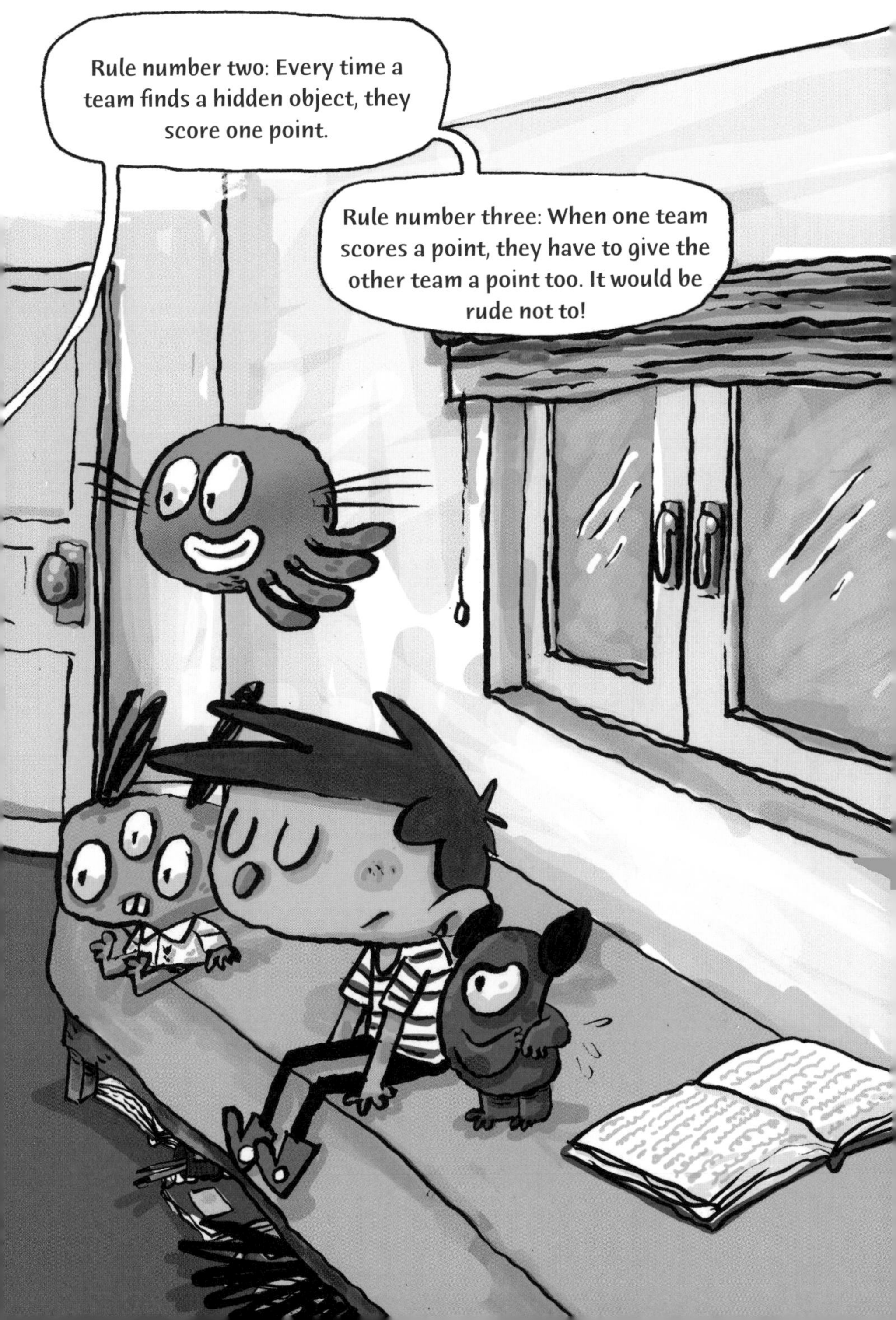
Rule number two: Every time a team finds a hidden object, they score one point.
Rule number three: When one team scores a point, they have to give the other team a point too. It would be rude not to!

But today, Brexfest isn't enough to take our minds off other things. We're too worried about Chef Roll and Krater to concentrate on the game. We breathe a sigh of relief when they're finally back in my room.

Of course I'm the perfect excuse! I can go to the restaurant, tell the owners I have to work on a project for school, and that I'd like to lend a hand. It's the perfect way to get the monsters into the restaurant. I can't believe my parents fall for such a far-fetched story about my school work.

Without further ado, I hurry back to the Nautilus with my bag on my back and, of course, all the monsters inside the hole in the bag. They don't want to miss a thing. Ody and Penelope, the restaurant owners, are happy I want to help. It's obvious they could use an extra pair of hands.

Ody and Penelope are very nice people, but their restaurant has seen better days. The decor is terrible and the menu is a mess. Mr. Flat is horrified.

All this mess is nothing compared to what we find in the kitchen. It's a complete disaster! Fortunately, Ody tells me that he and Penelope need to go out and run some errands. He asks me if I can look after the restaurant for a while.

5

Getting the Nautilus shipshape

As soon as we're alone at the Nautilus, we set about cleaning everything. It's shocking! Some of the junk must have been piling up for years. Fortunately, we had some good practice tidying up my room. Thanks to that, I think we manage to do a pretty good job.

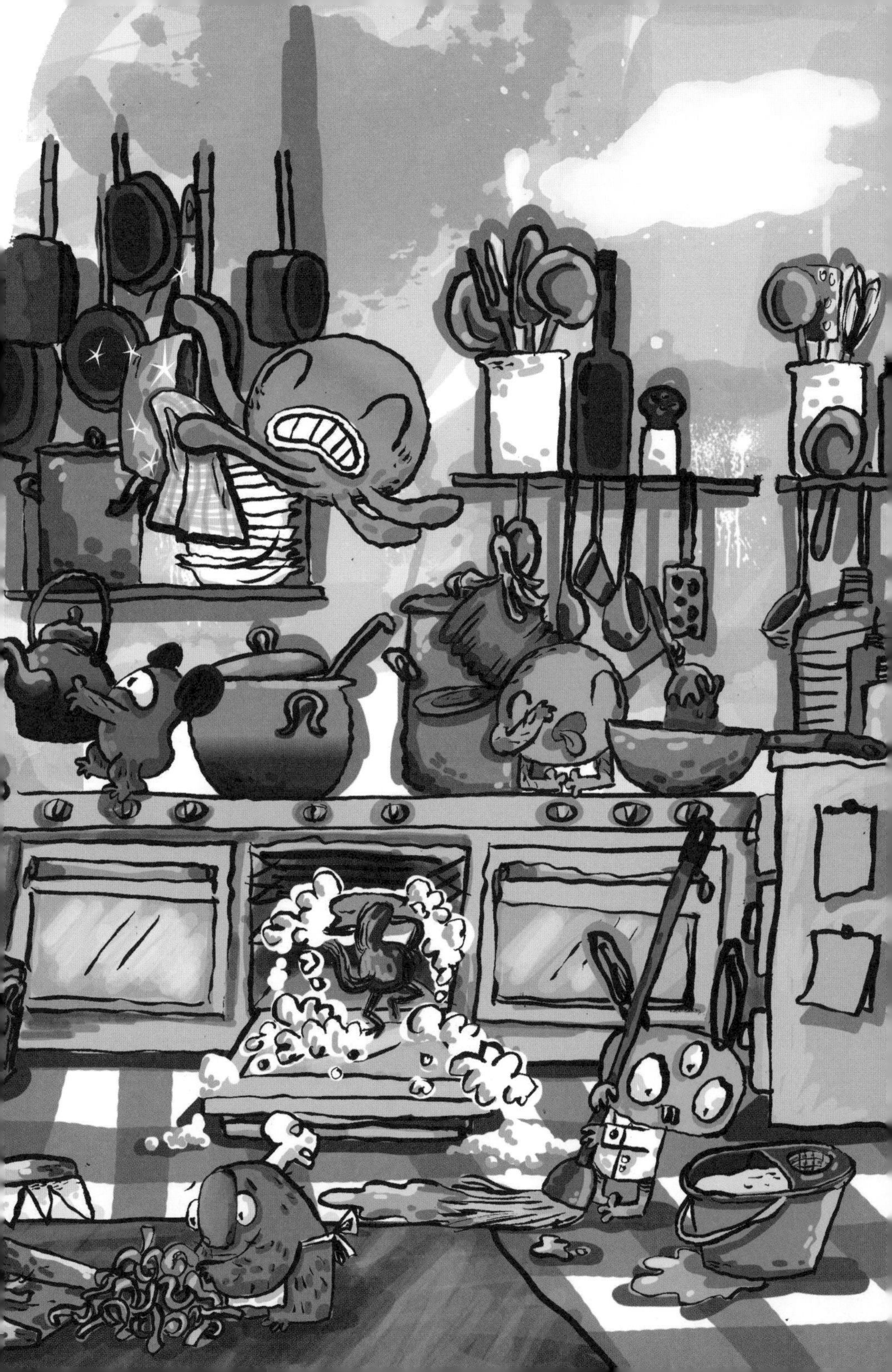

Pintaca thinks the restaurant sign is ugly, so she decides to give it a lick of paint.

The real challenge is in the kitchen, though. What a great big mess! There's so much to do! With Chef Roll barking orders at us, we get down to work. He tells us all what to do while he's writing a whole menu for the restaurant.

When the new menu is ready, Chef Roll starts to run the kitchen like a ship's captain.

Suddenly, we hear a terrifying scream. We turn around and look, and Penelope and Ody are standing in the doorway. They look as white as a sheet. Oh, no, they've seen the monsters!

Penelope and Ody have a hard time understanding what's happening. But the more I explain, the more they come around to the idea.

Maybe it's because we've spruced up their restaurant in record time, but Ody and Penelope soon realize that the monsters are quite friendly. When they eventually calm down, we get right back to work.

Chef Roll tries to show Penelope and Ody a thing or two, but they have a lot to learn.

It's a disaster! Jean-Paul Sorbet's going to eat us alive.

No! We have to convince him that the Nautilus is a good restaurant. And we have to get Dr. Brut to talk about our book! What has he done with it? Where is he hiding it? Any information at all will help!

It's going to take years to turn the Nautilus into a good restaurant!

Well, we only have two days left!

Arrrghhhh!!!!! One of the monsters has turned into lots of smaller ones!

Penelope is right. Seeing how much work there is to do, Drilox thinks he can be more useful by breaking up into an army of little Driloxes. And there they are, lots of little Driloxes, all busy cleaning the dining room.

Mr. Flat asks Penelope and Ody to keep the secret and not tell anyone that a gaggle of monsters is helping them out. They promise not to say a word.

After dinner, I shut myself into my room with my friends. We've worked so hard, we're exhausted now. But there's one thing we don't want to miss, and that's reading time! We choose *Charlie and the Chocolate Factory*, by Roald Dahl. All this talk of chocolate makes Chef Roll want to prepare some yummy hot chocolate for us.

During the night, I dream that I'm visiting Willy Wonka's chocolate factory. There, in the chocolate room, I find them all: Charlie, Mr. Wonka, Veruca, Mike, Violet, and Augustus, as well as the Oompa-Loompas, who are singing one of their songs at the top of their lungs. But the strangest thing is that I float through the chocolate room aboard the Nautilus, Captain Nemo's submarine. It feels like I'm travelling 20,000 leagues under the chocolate sea!

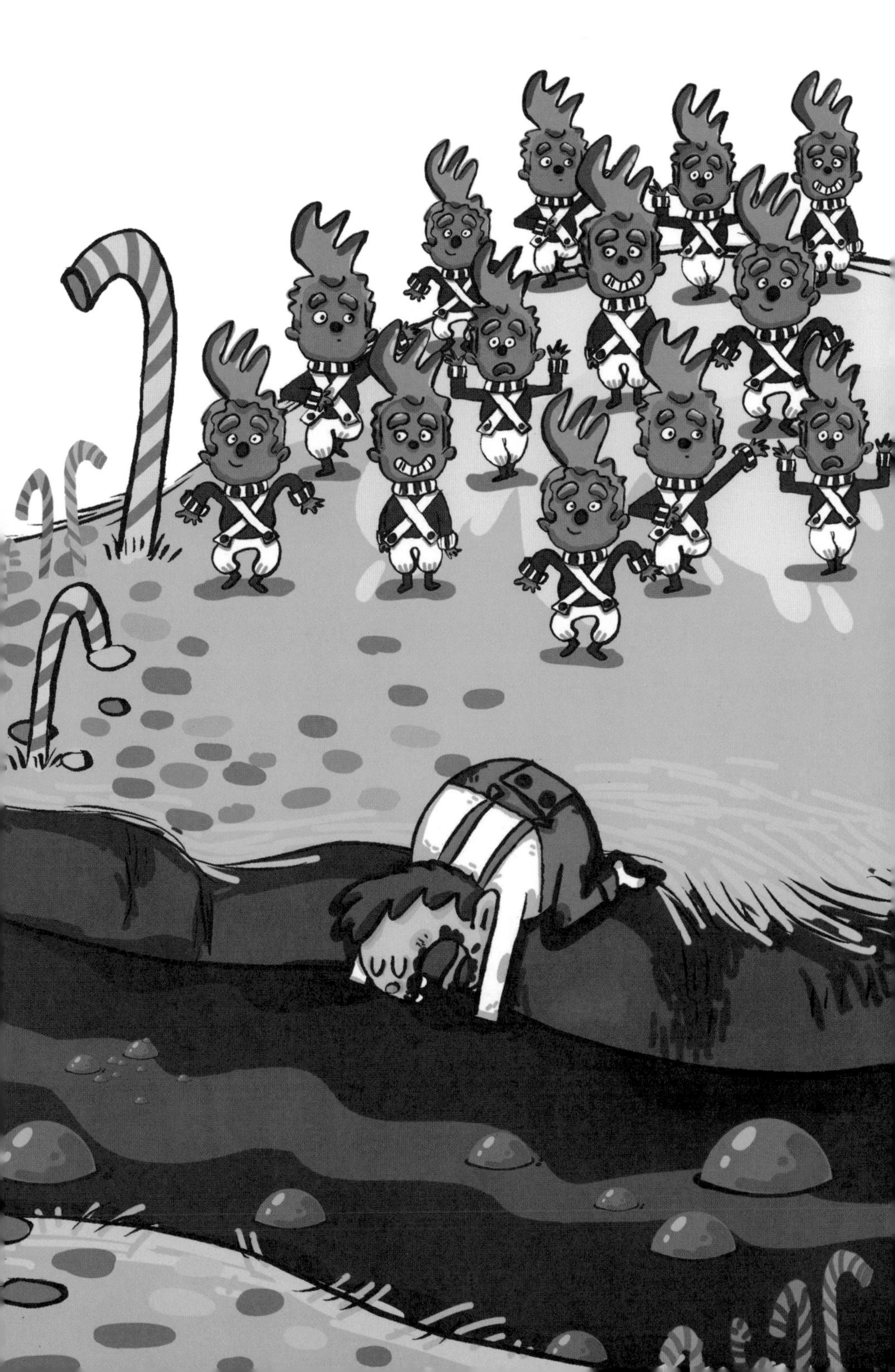

6

A little research goes a long way

When we wake up the next morning, we see that Brex has built a telescope from a pile of useless-looking things he found in my room. We can use the telescope to keep an eye on what Dr. Brut and Nabo are doing.

Dr. Brut really doesn't miss an opportunity to be horrible. We can't imagine what the birds in the park might have done to get him so worked up, but the nasty doctor is determined to chase them away.

It makes the monsters angry to see Dr. Brut bothering the birds.

My friends can't stand to see anything in trouble, whether it's a monster, a person, or a bird.

A few moments later, a very strange character is in the park, telling off Dr. Brut. By a stroke of good (or bad) luck, a police officer happens to pass by.

Dr. Brut is outraged when the officer writes him a ticket!

I can see now how nasty and completely crazy Dr. Brut is. But why? Why is he so nasty and so crazy? I look him up on the Internet, but I can't find anything. None of the monsters can explain it either.

Ziro's idea is fantastic! While the other monsters go off to work at the Nautilus, Ziro, Mr. Flat and I pay a visit to the public library. We look high and low, then we look even higher and even lower.

Mr. Flat and I scour the library in search of interesting books. Meanwhile, Ziro picks up a very big book called *Stories About Monsters and Other Creatures That Never Existed*. Then he starts to read it.

As Mr. Flat and I browse the books, we hear Ziro calling us. He's found what he was looking for. To find it, he had to go all the way to page 569! What that page says is crystal clear.

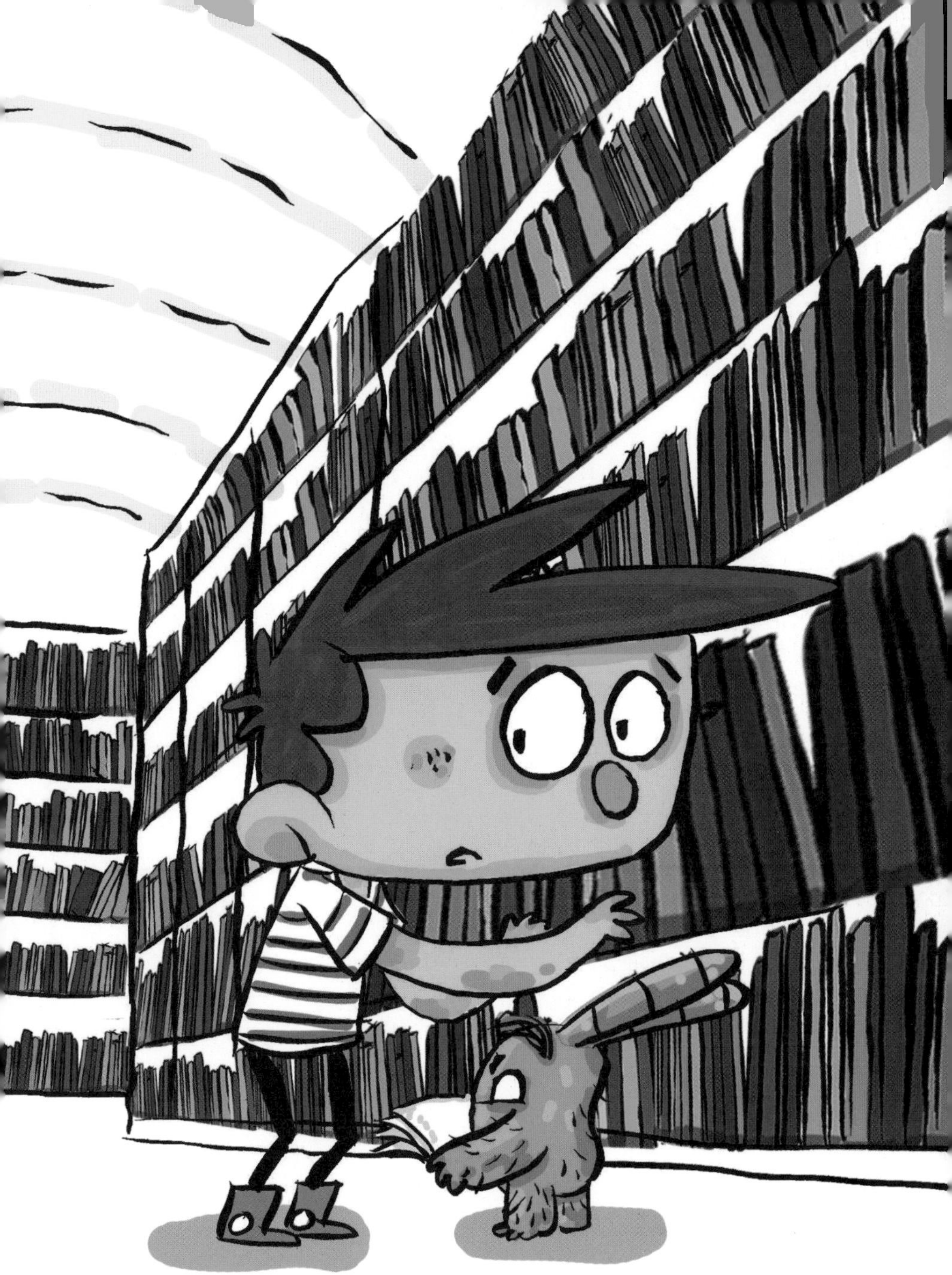

Brutali maximus

This very peculiar monster goes by the name of Dr. Brut. He is the very definition of evil. His motto is "Evil for evil's sake." It is said that Dr. Brut is responsible for many bad things that have happened in the monster and human worlds. It is largely due to his bad reputation that humans, and especially children, are afraid of monsters. Dr. Brut uses his human-like appearance to spread misery without anyone noticing. If you see him, do not go near him.

According to the ancient prophecies of the land of monsters, a boy and a select group of monsters will one day, after a thrilling series of adventures, manage to get the better of Dr. Brut. When that day comes, humans and monsters will finally be able to live together in peace and harmony.

I'm sure I don't need to tell you how scared we feel after reading what the book has to say about Dr. Brut. We've just learned he's well and truly a very nasty monster!

That night, before we pick up *Charlie and the Chocolate Factory* again, we have a lot to talk about. Those of us who went to the library tell the others what we found out about Dr. Brut. And then, Chef Roll, Brex, Pintaca, Emmo, Dr. Veter, Drilox, and Krater remind us there's still lots of work to be done at the Nautilus.

7

A dry run

In the morning, we go in to the Nautilus very early. We want to do a dry run to make sure everything goes as well as it possibly can the next day. Chef Roll is still worried, though.

We draw up a plan of the restaurant so we know exactly where we'll be seating Jean-Paul Sorbet, Dr. Brut, and the other customers.

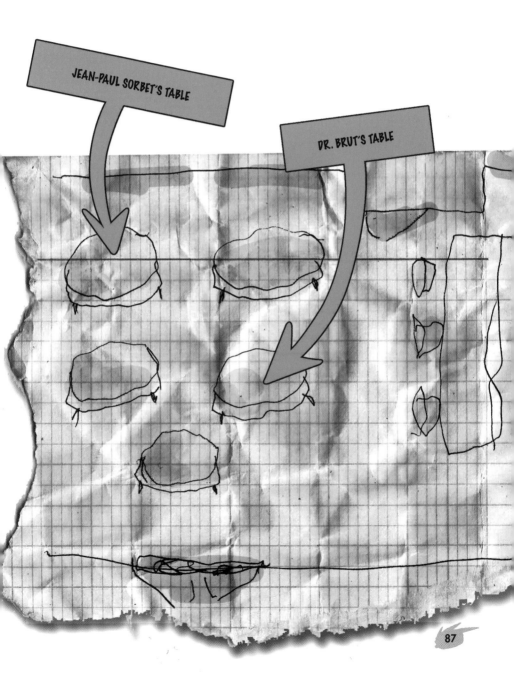

JEAN-PAUL SORBET'S TABLE

DR. BRUT'S TABLE

Once the plan is drawn up, Chef Roll tries to show Penelope and Ody four basic techniques for serving customers.

Obviously, seeing how clumsy Penelope and Ody are, we decide I should be the server. That way we can make sure neither of them go near Jean-Paul Sorbet's table, or Dr. Brut's. But will they fare any better in the kitchen?

What happens next in the kitchen is beyond explanation. I'm astounded to see how utterly useless Penelope and Ody really are.

We decide it's best that I serve Jean-Paul Sorbet's and Dr. Brut's tables myself, so that Penelope and Ody can serve the others. The monsters can stay in the kitchen and prepare the dishes under Chef Roll's orders. Emmo's going to stay by the coffee machine, so he looks like any other kitchen appliance.

Emmo has a bit of a short fuse, especially with Pintaca, but really, he's happy to help.

Penelope and Ody are both very nice people, but it's a tall order to think we're going to pull the whole thing off.

Over dinner, I tell my parents I'm going to spend the next day at the Nautilus too, to focus on my school work. At the same time, I can lend a hand to Penelope and Ody. But my parents have some news to tell me.

I tell the monsters my parents are going to come and eat at the restaurant. They try their best to calm me down, but they don't do a very good job.

The monsters are very stubborn. No matter what happens, they refuse to go to bed without reading. Not a day without a line!

Tonight, Mr. Flat chooses an extract from *The Odyssey*, by Homer. According to him, even though it's a poem, together with *The Iliad*, it's considered to be the first great work in the history of literature.

What a story! In the extract Mr. Flat has chosen, Polyphemus the Cyclops takes Odysseus and his companions prisoner in a cave so he can eat them later. Odysseus makes the giant one-eyed creature believe his name is Nobody. It's his way of tricking Polyphemus, because when Odysseus attacks the giant, he shouts for help from the other Cyclops, but he says, "Nobody hurt me!" Of course, the other Cyclops do nothing to help. The next day, Odysseus and his companions manage to escape by hiding in a flock of sheep that have been sleeping in Polyphemus's cave.

Odysseus was so brave!

Yes, my dear, but Odysseus isn't brave because he's strong, he's brave because he's smart. And because he knows how to use his words!

What a coincidence! Odysseus, that sounds like our friend Ody at the Nautilus.

That's why he's often called "clever Odysseus."

What a coincidence! Nautilus was the name of Captain Nemo's submarine!

8

The moment
of truth

The moment of truth is coming and, to be honest, I start to get the jitters. Seeing all the monsters so determined to make this work, I'm afraid to be afraid. Yes, I know it's strange to say I'm afraid to be afraid, but that's the way it is.

Are you afraid, Alex?

Errrrr ... Yes!

Good. So are we. Only a fool wouldn't be scared. Look at Ziro!

He's more scared than the rest of us, because he's the one who thinks the most!

And so, with our hearts in our mouths, we set off for the Nautilus. When we get there, Mr. Flat's flair for organization and Chef Roll's kitchen orders soon put us to work.

Chef Roll makes sure everything is ready first.

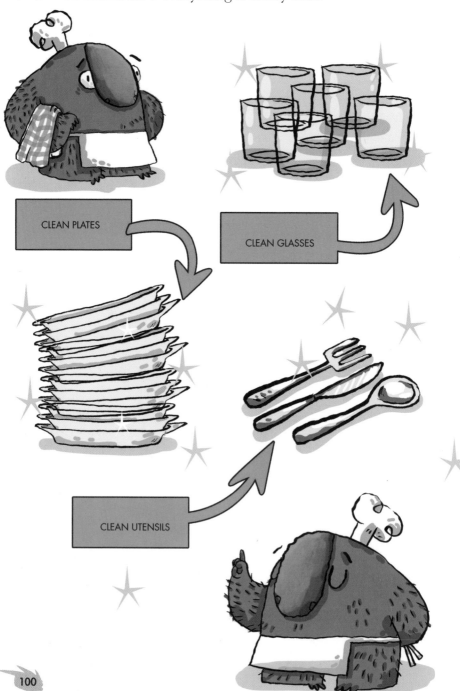

CLEAN PLATES

CLEAN GLASSES

CLEAN UTENSILS

Next, he lines us all up for inspection.

The strangest thing happens when we open the restaurant. Of all the customers in the world who could come to the Nautilus, the first ones through the door are Lidia Lines and her dad.

As soon as I've taken the order for Lidia and her dad, the next customers arrive: my parents! What a nightmare!

My bad luck is far from running out, because the next customer to come in is Emma, the school librarian. Aren't there any other restaurants open around here?

And then, Jean-Paul Sorbet walks in! He's even more obnoxious than his photo in the newspaper suggests.

In the kitchen, the monsters are working like crazy! It's a little chaotic, but they're doing a great job!

We're so busy, we nearly forget. But suddenly, the moment of truth is here. And it has a name: Dr. Brut.

9

Let the fun and games begin!

We manage to keep things pretty much under control even though Jean-Paul Sorbet is driving us crazy with his demands. He wants to taste everything the Nautilus has on the menu. But things start to get seriously out of hand with Dr. Brut around. As soon as he starts complaining, it doesn't escape Jean-Paul Sorbet's attention.

As rudely as only he knows how, Jean-Paul Sorbet screams and shouts to get his own way. Then I have an idea.

Dr. Brut finds it terribly amusing to see that our efforts are about to lay an egg.

Obviously, my parents and the other customers are a little perplexed to see Jean-Paul Sorbet screaming his head off and Dr. Brut cackling like an evil villain.

That's when something happens that we could have never predicted. I bring Dr. Brut and Nabo the fish they ordered, and as soon as I show it to them …

Dr. Brut's fish flies through the air and lands right on Jean-Paul Sorbet's forehead. His glass of wine then spills all over my mom. Caught by surprise, my mom knocks over her bowl of soup right into Lidia's dad's lap, and a second later the Nautilus plunges into total chaos.

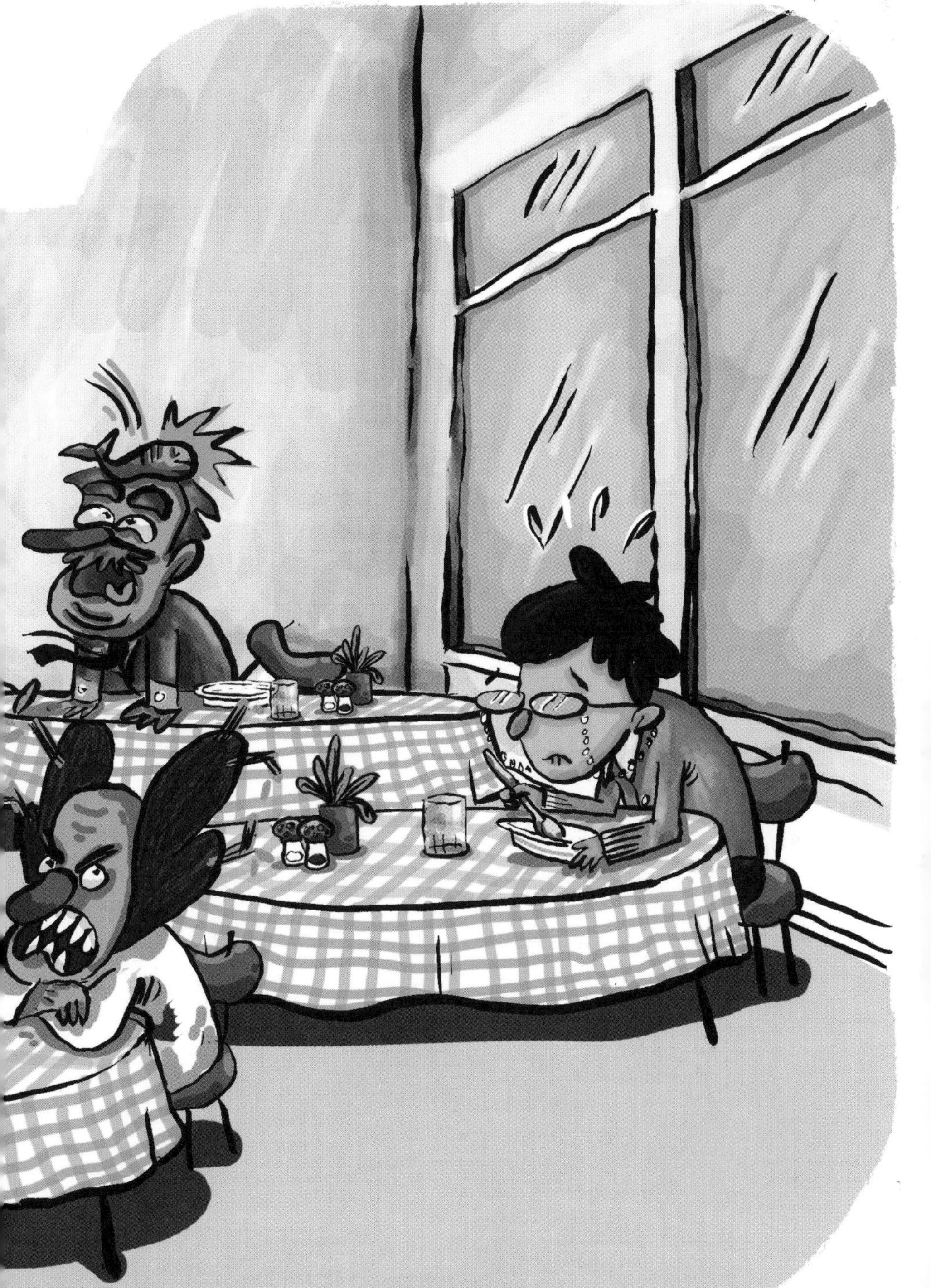

All that's missing now are the monsters! Everyone starts to scream, the customers because they're seeing monsters, the monsters because they like to scream, and Jean-Paul Sorbet because he's horrified by it all. Things couldn't get any worse! And in all the madness, Chef Roll manages to knock over the ice cream cart and starts raving about the desserts.

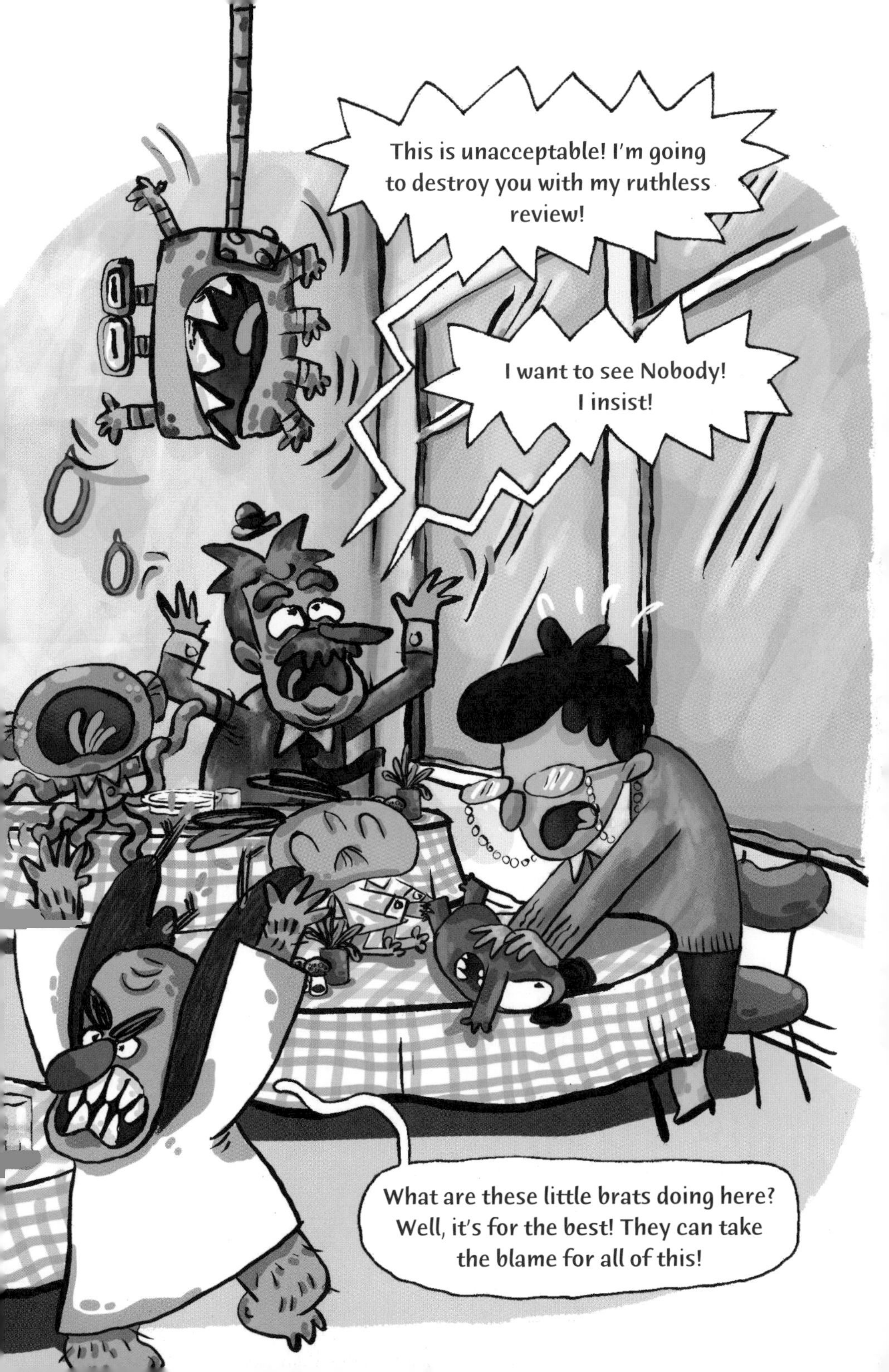
This is unacceptable! I'm going to destroy you with my ruthless review!
I want to see Nobody! I insist!
What are these little brats doing here? Well, it's for the best! They can take the blame for all of this!

Just as I think the situation can't get any worse, Mr. Flat barks an order and Dr. Brut runs away as fast as his legs will carry him.

Suddenly, Emmo opens his mouth and floods us all with a powerful bright light.

When Emmo's light beam goes out, the monsters are already hidden safely in my bag and everyone looks a little lost. Now's the time to improvise a little.

10

Was it really that bad?

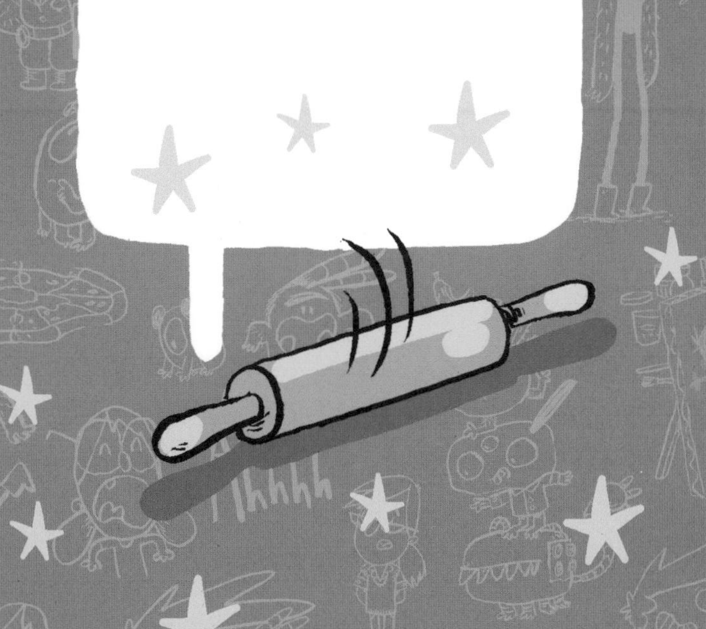

After I help clean the restaurant, I go home. What a disaster! With the terrible review Jean-Paul Sorbet is sure to write, I'm worried the Nautilus is going to have to close its doors. It looks like Dr. Brut's plan has succeeded. And as for the dish I'm supposed to take to school tomorrow, I don't have anything. Nothing at all!

My parents try to make me feel better. They tell me it's not my fault, that sometimes things don't go the way we want them to.

So I go to my room, where I'm expecting to find lots of very sad monsters.

But I see nothing of the sort. None of the monsters are sad at all! In fact, there's a party in my room! It's incredible how happy they all are. They're singing, they're dancing, and I can't even begin to understand why!

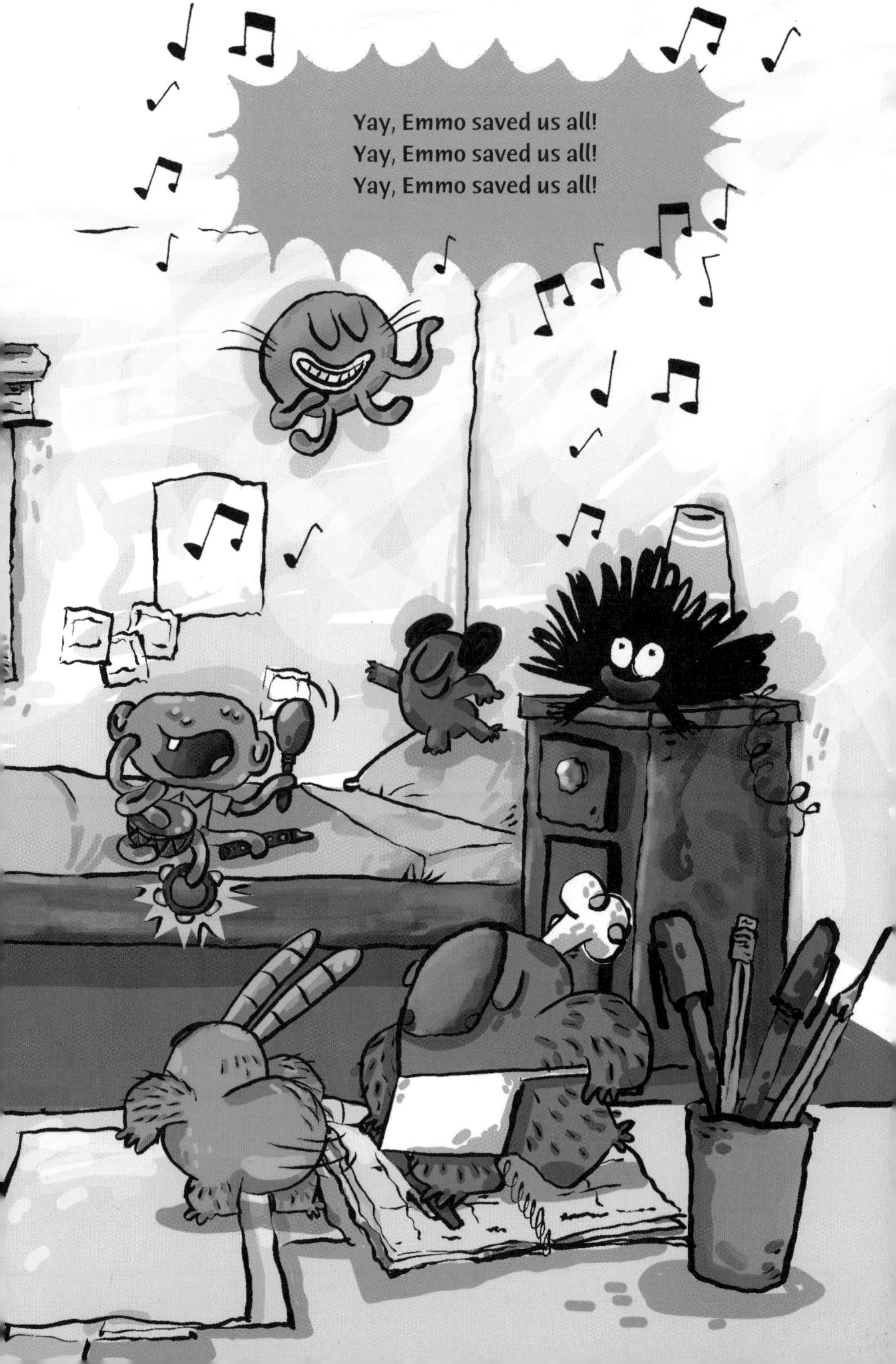
Yay, Emmo saved us all!
Yay, Emmo saved us all!
Yay, Emmo saved us all!

I try to explain to the monsters that we failed. But then they explain to me how they see it.

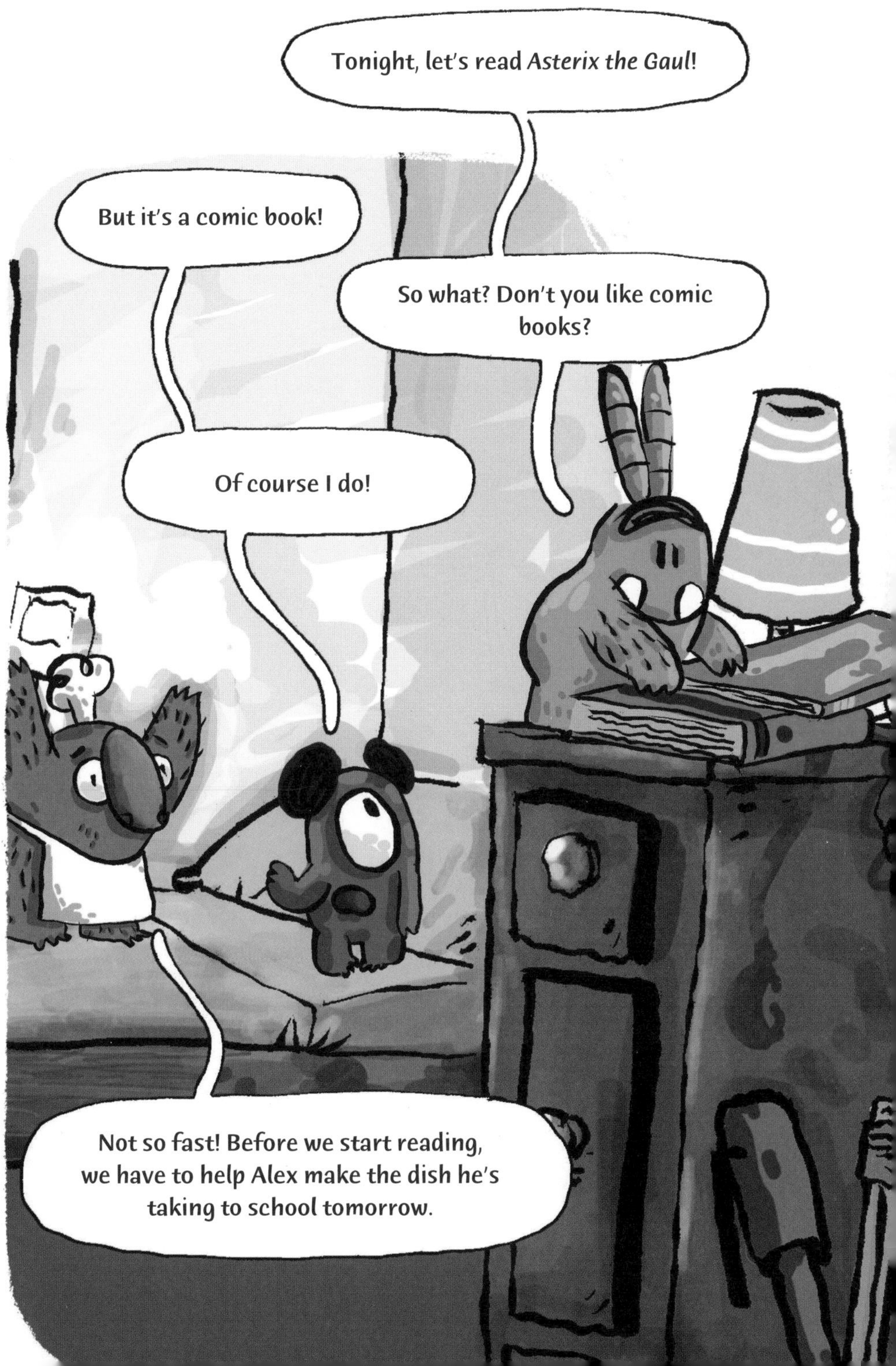
Tonight, let's read *Asterix the Gaul*!
But it's a comic book!
So what? Don't you like comic books?
Of course I do!
Not so fast! Before we start reading, we have to help Alex make the dish he's taking to school tomorrow.

Thanks to Emmo, who has turned himself into a kitchen counter, Chef Roll shows me how to make a super easy dish, right here in my room. He says this recipe was always a winner with the other monsters when they lived in *The Book of Monsters*.

To make Chef Roll's super special sandwich rolls …

all we need is …

some sliced bread, some ham, and some cheese.

First you flatten the bread with a rolling pin.

Then you put the ham and cheese on the bread.

Roll it all up, and then for the finishing touch …

just slice the sandwich roll into little wheels.

That night, we laugh as we read all about the adventures of Asterix and Obelix, the magic potion, Obelix's menhirs and wild boar, and the battles between the Gauls in the village and the Romans lost in the forest.

11

We did it!

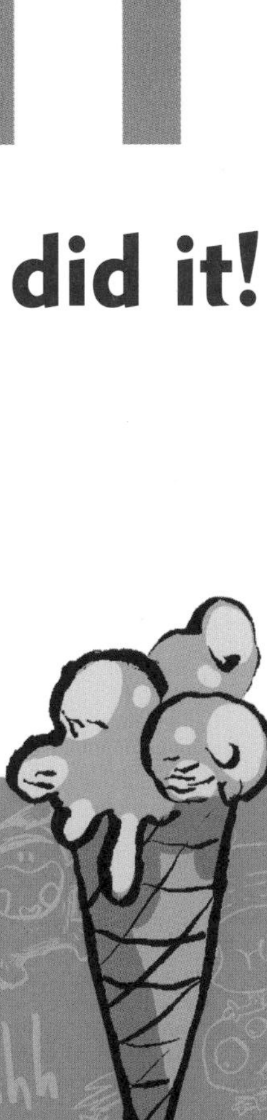

The next day, all the monsters want to come to school with me to see how everyone likes the super special sandwich rolls Chef Roll taught me to make. I don't have the strength to say no.

Of course, because it's time to go to school, I run into Lidia on my way out the door.

At recess, we all unveil our dishes and put them out on our desks. Before we taste them, we vote for whose has the best presentation. I can't help but feel a little disappointed.

I don't know why, though, because when the time comes to taste the food, everyone, and I mean absolutely everyone, dives right in to my sandwich rolls.

Before they've all gone, I save one of my little sandwich wheels for Emma. It's the least I can do. Every week, she selects a stack of books for me to take home. What's more, she didn't even get to eat dessert at the Nautilus!

… and that's how Jean-Paul Sorbet ended up with egg on his face.

Why are you laughing, Emma?

On the radio, the host has been making fun of that weird restaurant critic Jean-Paul Sorbet. He wrote a terrible review about Nobody's restaurant. He said: "Nobody is a terrible cook. Nobody is an absolute disaster in the kitchen." What an idiot!

The monsters are laughing so hard, my backpack starts shaking. I have to go before Emma notices. So far, the day has been going pretty well, and things get even better on my way home at the end of the afternoon. We come across a long line-up on the street and decide to join it to see where it leads.

I can't believe my eyes. Penelope and Ody have turned the Nautilus into an ice cream shop. And the line-up for ice cream is never-ending.

Penelope and Ody tell me there'll always be ice cream for me and my friends at the Nautilus. I ask them which friends they're talking about. And they repeat that there'll always be ice cream for me and the others, no matter who I'm with.

It's so strange. Other than how popular my dish was at school, I get the feeling everything else was an epic fail. But all the monsters, as well as Penelope and Ody, see things differently.

And suddenly, for no apparent reason, I realize something: Emmo's light beam erased the memory of everyone who saw the monsters! But what about me? I remember everything. How can that be? Did the monsters know it wouldn't affect me?

That night, we devour Penelope's and Ody's ice cream. It's so delicious! After our little snack, the monsters start singing the same song I heard the day before. This time I join in, because now I see exactly what they mean. We did it!

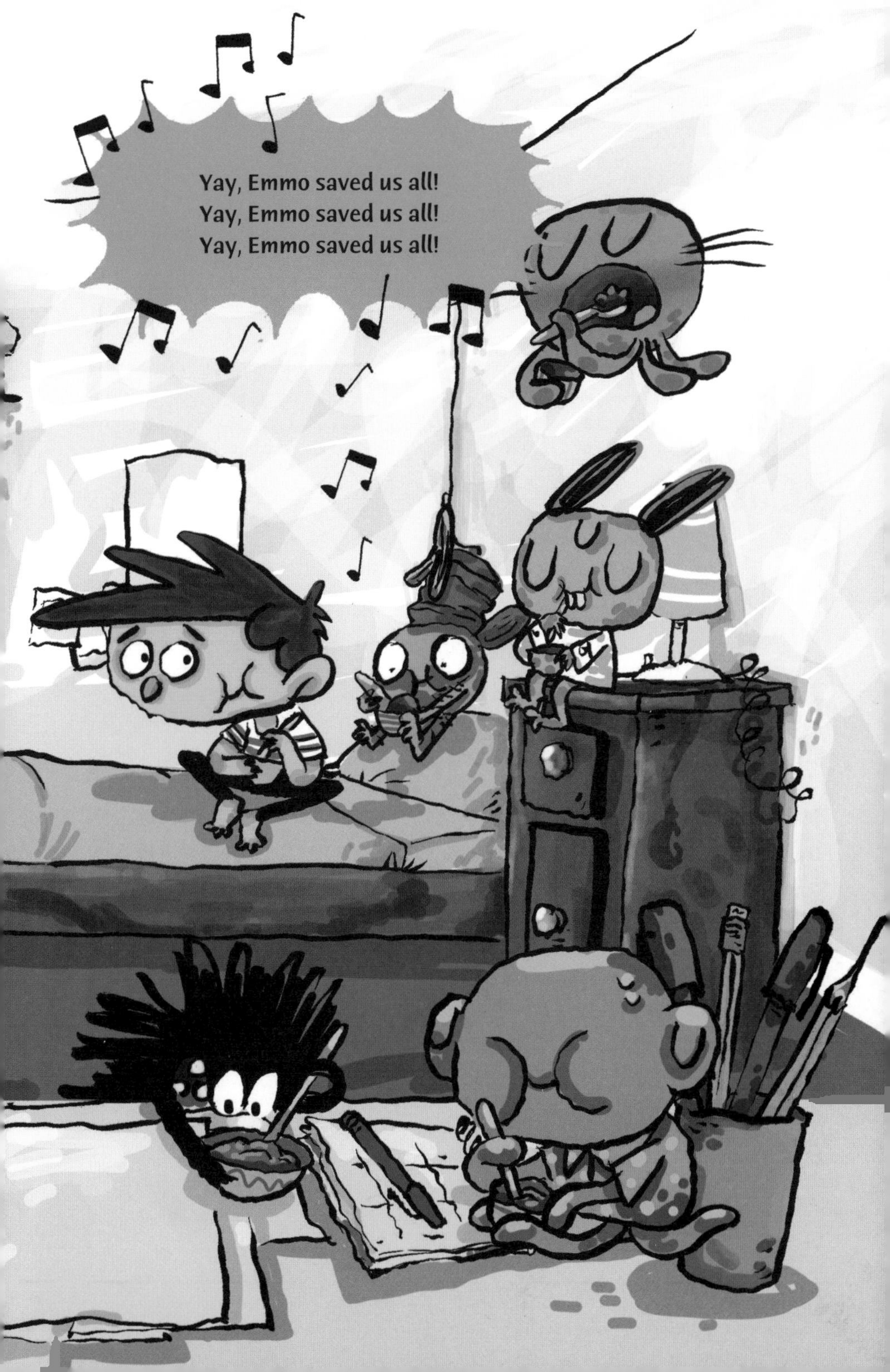
Yay, Emmo saved us all!
Yay, Emmo saved us all!
Yay, Emmo saved us all!

Original title: Salvem el Nautilus!
© 2014, Combel Editorial, S.A.
© 2014, Jaume Copons
© 2014, Liliana Fortuny

© 2018 CHOUETTE PUBLISHING (1987) INC.

CrackBoom! Books is an imprint of Chouette Publishing (1987) Inc.

Text: Jaume Copons
Illustrations: Liliana Fortuny
Translated from the French by David Warriner

Chouette Publishing would like to thank the Government of Canada and SODEC
for their financial support.

Bibliothèque et Archives nationales du Québec and Library and Archives Canada
cataloguing in publication

Copons, Jaume, 1966-

[Salvem el Nautilus! English]

Restaurant Rescue!

(Alex and the monsters)
Translation of: À la rescousse du restaurant, which is a French translation of:
Salvem el Nautilus!
For children aged 7 and up.

ISBN 978-2-924786-10-9 (flexibound cover)

I. Fortuny, Liliana. II. Warriner, David. III. Title. IV. Title: Salvem el Nautilus!
English.

PZ7.C66Re 2018   j849'.936   C2017-941615-4

Printed in China
10 9 8 7 6 5 4 3 2 1   CHO2023 DEC2017

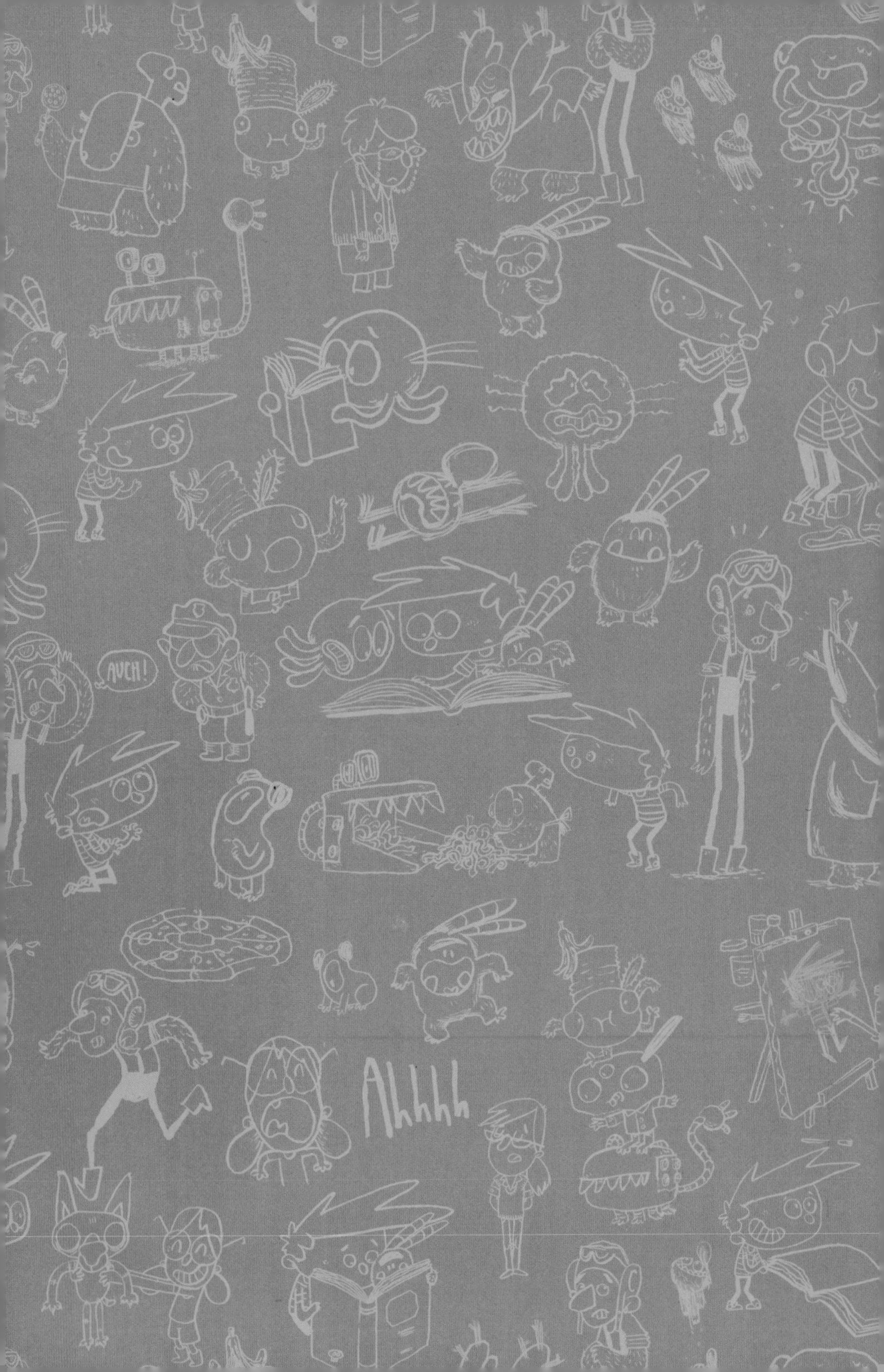
AUCH!
Ahhhh